I Lost My Kisses

For Daniel, Andrew, and Adam, the best kissers in the world.
— T. T.

For Jo.
— N. B.

Text copyright © 2007 by Trudie Trewin
Illustrations copyright © 2007 by Nick Bland
First published in Australia in 2007 by Scholastic Australia.

Library of Congress Cataloging-in-Publication Data is available
ISBN-13: 978-0-545-05557-4
ISBN-10: 0-545-05557-1

10 9 8 7 6 5 4 3 2 1   03 04 05 06 07

Printed in Malaysia
First Orchard Books edition, January 2008
Art done in watercolor and graphite pencil.

Cover illustration copyright © 2008 by Nick Bland
This edition design by Patty Harris

Library of Congress Cataloging-in-Publication Data
Trewin, Trudie. I lost my kisses / Trudie Trewin ; illustrations by Nick Bland. — 1st Orchard Books ed.   p. cm.
Summary: Matilda Rose loves to kiss hello, goodbye, good morning, and goodnight, but on the day her father is to return from a trip,
she cannot find her kisses anywhere, despite knowing how they feel, taste, and sound.
ISBN-13: 978-0-545-05557-4 (reinforced bdg.)
ISBN-10: 0-545-05557-1
[1. Kissing— Fiction. 2. Lost and found possessions— Fiction. 3. Family life— Fiction.] I. Bland, Nick, 1973- ill. II. Title.
PZ7.T332Ial 2008 [E] — dc22 2007030687

I Lost My Kisses

BY TRUDIE TREWIN

ILLUSTRATED BY NICK BLAND

Orchard Books / New York

An Imprint of Scholastic Inc.

Matilda Rose loves to kiss.

She kisses hello. She kisses good-bye.

She kisses good morning and she kisses good night.

But today Matilda Rose feels bad.

"Something is terribly, horribly wrong," cries Matilda. "I lost my kisses!"

"Don't be silly, Matilda Rose," says her mother. "They'll be there when you need them."

"But I need them today!" says Matilda. "Daddy is coming home. And the first thing he always says is 'Where's my big smoocheroo?' I just have to find my kisses!"

"Maybe I lost them in my bedroom."

Matilda wanders through her house, singing, "Kisses, kisses, come back to me. I lost my kisses—now where can they be?"

"What do kisses look like?" asks her friend Lambkins.

"I don't know," says Matilda. "But I do know what they feel like. They can be soft like Mommy's sweet-dreams-kiss, or ticklish like Daddy's whisker-kiss."

Matilda looks in her toy basket and under her bed,
but all she finds is an old banana.

"Yuck!" She sighs. "I will never find my kisses."

"Maybe I lost them outside," says Matilda,
and she goes to the garden shouting,
"Kisses, kisses, come back to me.
I lost my kisses—now where can they be?"
Matilda sits down. "Cuddles, have you seen
my kisses?"

"What do kisses look like?" he asks.

"I don't know," says Matilda. "But I do
know what they taste like. They can be
yummy like a chocolaty candy-kiss."

Matilda swings high in the treetops
to look in a bird's nest.

She peeks down the well, but all she
finds is her long-lost doll.

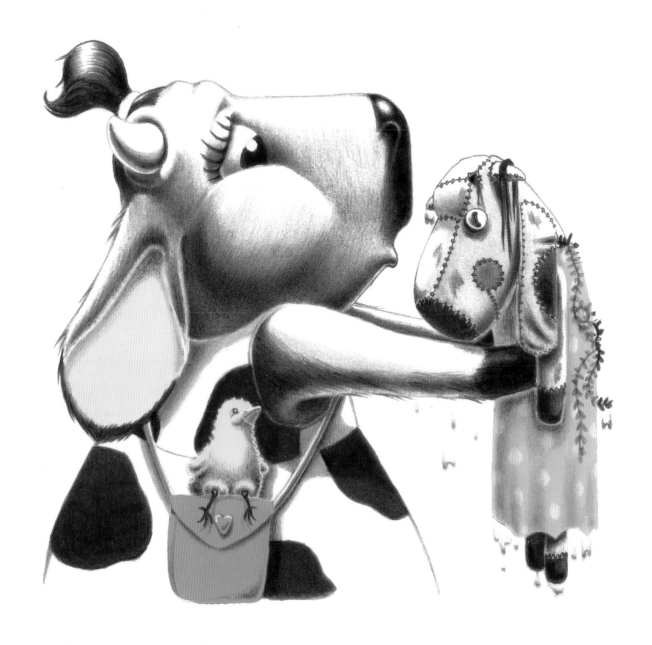

"Oh, Dolly, I'm so glad to see you! I could kiss you!"
says Matilda.

"Except I lost my kisses," she adds sadly.

Later that morning, Matilda goes shopping
with her mom and baby brother, Nate.

Maybe I can find my kisses here, she thinks.

"Can I help you?" asks the grocer, Mr. McSnortie.

"Yes!" exclaims Matilda. "I am looking for my kisses."

"What do kisses look like?" asks Mr. McSnortie.

"I don't know," says Matilda. "But I do know what they sound like. They can make a little *mwa* sound like a kiss-it-better-kiss. Or a wet, slurpy, sloppy sound like baby Nate's slobber-kiss."

Matilda searches and searches.
She looks in the cereal boxes and behind the milk.
But she cannot find her kisses anywhere.

Matilda checks the mailbox on the way home.
She has looked everywhere, and she still
hasn't found one single kiss.
And Daddy is arriving very soon.

At the airport, Matilda sits down and waits.

When everyone starts getting off the plane, she does not even look up.

But she hears them kissing.

It seems that everyone has kisses—everyone except her.

A big tear slides down Matilda's cheek.

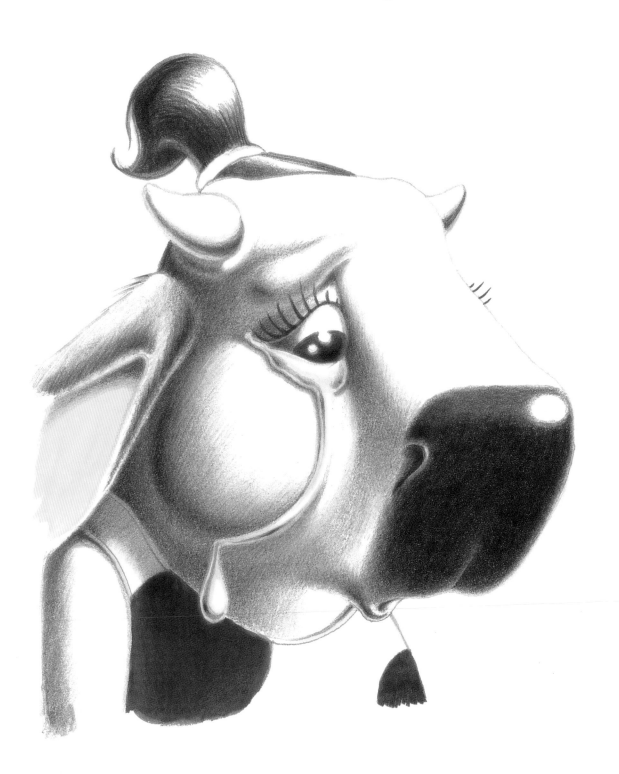

Suddenly she hears a booming voice.

"Matilda Rose, where's my big smoocheroo?"

Matilda feels something deep inside her heart.
A stretching feeling! Almost a bursting feeling!

Matilda gives Daddy the biggest smoocheroo!

"My goodness, Matilda Rose," says Daddy.
"That's the best kiss ever."

Matilda smiles.

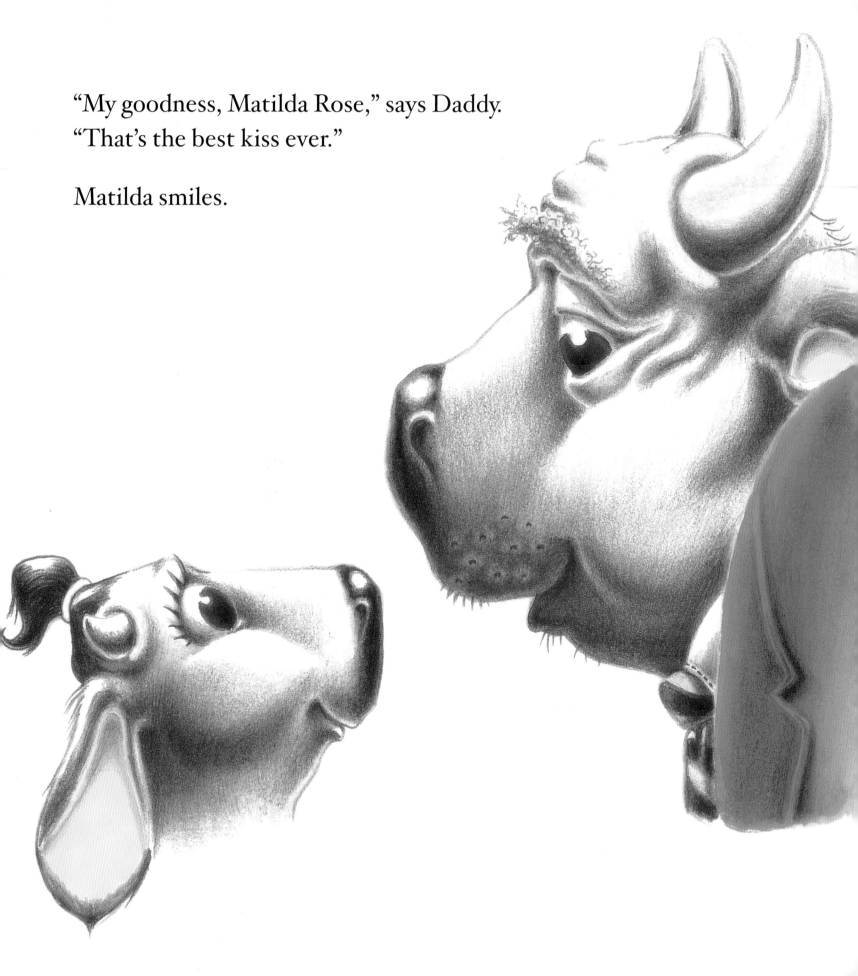

"*Mwa.*"